Eva
the Enchanted
Ball Fairy

Special thanks to
Sue Mongredien

ISBN 978-0-545-43396-9

Eva
the Enchanted
Ball Fairy

by Daisy Meadows

SCHOLASTIC INC.

New York   Toronto   London   Auckland
Sydney   Mexico City   New Delhi   Hong Kong

The Fairyland Palace

The Orangery

The Lake

Maze

Petting Zoo

PETTING ZOO

Garden

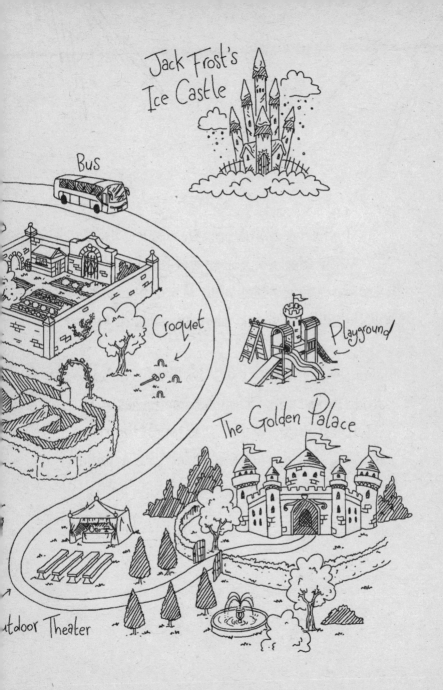

Jack Frost's
Ice Castle

Bus

Croquet

Playground

The Golden Palace

Outdoor Theater

The fairies are planning a magical ball,
With guests of honor and fun for all.
They're expecting a night full of laughter and cheer,
But they'll get a shock when my goblins appear!

Adventures and treats will be things of the past,
And I'll beat those troublesome fairies at last.
My iciest magic will blast through the room
And the world will be plunged into grimness
and gloom!

Contents

A Dancing Disaster

"One-two-three, one-two-three, one-two-three," murmured Rachel Walker under her breath, trying to concentrate on what her feet were doing. She and her best friend, Kirsty Tate, were staying at the Golden Palace for a Royal Sleepover Camp. Today, they were in the ballroom, enjoying a dance lesson.

The ballroom was beautiful, with huge sparkly chandeliers hanging from the ceiling, and dark-red wallpaper that looked like velvet.

It was the last full day of the camp and Kirsty and Rachel had had lots of fun. They'd been on a treasure hunt, taken part in a field day and a pageant, enjoyed a tea party in the palace gardens, and much more. It had been so exciting to stay in a real palace with a drawbridge, moat, and gold-topped towers. Best of all, the girls had also found themselves on more wonderful fairy adventures, this time with the Princess Fairies!

A grand ball was taking place that evening, and everyone was planning on dressing up in their nicest clothes. Louis

and Caroline, the directors who had
looked after the campers all week, were
teaching them the waltz, but nobody
was finding it easy.

"Whoops," said one boy, accidentally
stepping on his partner's toes.

"Sorry," said a girl as she swung
around too quickly and bumped into the
person behind her.

"Ow," said Kirsty as she stumbled, knocking against one of the tables at the far end of the room. The table had been decorated with flower arrangements and elegant glass vases filled with colorful candy, ready for the ball that evening. One of the vases fell over, and Kirsty barely caught it before it hit the floor. "Oh, dear," Louis said with a sigh as he exchanged glances with Caroline. "This isn't going as well as I'd hoped."

Kirsty and Rachel looked at each other, too. They had a good idea why everyone was finding it so hard to learn the waltz—it was all because of Jack Frost!

At the beginning of the week, the girls had been magically whisked away to Fairyland, where a special ball was being held in honor of the seven Princess Fairies. But mean Jack Frost had turned up uninvited with his goblins. He stole the Princess Fairies' magic tiaras and took them to the human world!

The Princess Fairies usually used their magic to look after all kinds of things—costumes, fun and games, adventures, and happiness—but without their tiaras, their magic wasn't working and normally fun times were turning into extraordinary disasters!

Luckily, Queen Titania had been able to cast a spell to make sure that the seven tiaras ended up in the Golden Palace. Ever since then, Kirsty and Rachel had been tracking them down. They'd found six of the stolen tiaras, but there was still one missing—the one that belonged to Princess Eva the Enchanted Ball Fairy.

"Unless we find Princess Eva's tiara, tonight's ball is going to be a disaster," Rachel whispered to Kirsty. "We have to keep an eye out for it."

Kirsty nodded, just as Caroline turned off the music and clapped her hands for silence. "I'm afraid we're out of time for our dance class," she said. "Don't worry if you're not sure about the steps yet—we'll still have plenty of fun at the ball later."

All the kids left the ballroom and started to make their way upstairs to get changed for the ball. Kirsty and Rachel hurried up the main staircase to the tower where they were sharing a bedroom.

"I'm going to wear the party dress that Phoebe the Fashion Fairy made me," Kirsty said as they walked along.

"Me too!" Rachel said, smiling.

They'd helped Phoebe and her friends the Party Fairies during another vacation, and Phoebe had rewarded each of the girls with a beautiful new dress. Even though both girls had grown taller since then, their dresses still fit perfectly, as if there was magic sewn into the seams.

Up in their bedroom, Rachel pulled open the wardrobe doors—and the girls were in for a horrible surprise. Kirsty's pink dress had a dark stain down the front that hadn't been there before, and Rachel's lilac dress had a large rip in one of the sleeves.

"Oh, no!" Kirsty exclaimed. "Our dresses look more like Cinderella's rags than beautiful ball gowns. What are we going to do?"

Flight to Fairyland

Just then, the girls heard a rustling sound—and out of the wardrobe flew a tiny blond fairy! She was wearing a glittery pink ball gown that billowed elegantly around her, and lilac shoes that were decorated with tiny jewels. The girls smiled as they recognized Princess Eva the Enchanted Ball Fairy.

"Hello," Princess Eva said, smiling. Then her face fell as she saw the ruined dresses. "Oh, dear," she said. "You can't wear *those* to the ball. If only I had my tiara, I could use its magic powers to make the dresses as good as new for you."

"We can wear something else," Kirsty said, turning away from the ruined dresses. "But more important, we can help you look for your tiara."

"Definitely," Rachel agreed. "We know that Jack Frost and his goblins are hiding in one of the towers. Why don't we search around there?"

"Thank you," Princess Eva replied.
"First, let me turn you into fairies.
Then we can fly up there together."
She waved her wand and a stream of
rainbow-colored sparkles swirled out,
twirling all around the girls. In the next
moment, they felt themselves shrinking
smaller and smaller until they were the
same size as Eva—and had their own
glittery fairy wings, too!

Kirsty grinned
as she fluttered
her wings and
swooped
around the
room. Being a
fairy was the
best thing
ever!

"Let's go," Eva said, and led them out of the room and toward the old tower that Jack Frost had made his hideout. They all flew up the spiral staircase  together, high above the crumbling stone steps. As they got near the top of the tower, the air grew much colder and icicles appeared on the walls.

"Hmmm," Eva said, a worried expression on her face. "It looks like Jack Frost is up to something. I think it must be his icy magic that has caused the temperature to drop so low. Come on, let's investigate."

At the top of the staircase, there was a

large wooden door that was slightly ajar.
The three fairies peeked around it to see
Jack Frost and his goblins inside. Swirls
of icy-blue magic crackled all around
them. Jack Frost was wearing Eva's
tiara as he addressed the goblins. "Good
news!" he cackled. "The spell cast by
Queen Titania
that kept all the
Princess Fairies'
tiaras at the
Golden
Palace is
wearing off.
So we can
take this
tiara to my
Ice Castle,"
he announced in a smug tone, "and

we'll have the most amazing ball
ever—way better than a silly fairy
ball."

With that, he clapped his hands, and
the icy-blue magic seemed to dance
around him and the goblins with a
fizzing sound. There was a sudden
shower of ice chips . . . and then he and
the goblins vanished.

"We'll have to go after them," Rachel said. "We need to get that tiara back!"

"Yes," Eva said. "And there's no time to spare. To Fairyland!" She waved her wand and more of the rainbow-colored sparkles burst around the fairies, whirling them out of the tower and away.

When the magic whirlwind slowed and lowered the three fairies to the ground, Kirsty, Rachel,

and Eva found themselves outside Jack
Frost's Ice Castle in Fairyland. It was
a forbidding place, extremely cold and
made of glittering blue ice. But as the
girls peeked through the windows into
the great hall, they realized that today
everything seemed much happier.

Jack Frost was busy preparing for his
ball. He raised his hand, firing an icy
bolt of magic — and in the next instant,
blue and green decorations appeared
around the room. *Zap!* There went
another icy bolt, making silver trays
appear on a table, piled high with ice
pops and lots of ice cream.

Zap! Ballroom music started playing.
With a final wave of his hand, Jack
Frost zapped an outfit for himself—an
ice-blue dress coat and
bow tie. He was still
wearing Eva's magic
tiara, Rachel noticed.
As the fairies
watched, the goblins
began pouring into
the room, all wearing
their party clothes.
"Let the Ice Castle
ball begin!" Jack
Frost declared, and
the goblins cheered.
But before long,
things started to go
wrong. Kirsty put her hands over her

ears as the music changed to horrible banging sounds. The ice cream and ice pops started melting into sticky globs on the silver trays. A sudden gust of wind blew the decorations off the walls, and the goblins' clothes suddenly looked tattered and torn. Jack Frost tried to get everyone dancing to the awful music, but the goblins didn't want to. Instead, they began pushing one another around and jumping on the tables.

Eva winced as the music banged and crashed even more loudly. "Jack Frost might think he can have the perfect ball because he has my tiara, but he's wrong," she said. "Unless I have the tiara, no one—not even Jack Frost—can have a successful ball."

"Oh, dear," Rachel said. "Look at him now. He's furious!"

Jack Frost stamped his foot in rage. "This is not good enough," he yelled. "I wanted a real ball—with elegant outfits, beautiful decorations, lovely music, and graceful dancing. Nothing has gone right.

This fairy tiara is broken!"

"I wonder . . ." said Rachel
thoughtfully to herself. "Yes, that might
work. . . ."

"What might work?" Kirsty asked.

Rachel smiled, her eyes shining. "I
have an idea," she said. "If Jack Frost
wants the perfect ball — then we'll give
him one!"

Flying Ice Cream

Rachel explained her plan. "Eva, if you could use some magic to disguise me as a party planner, I might be able to get into the Ice Castle. I can pretend I'm there to help Jack Frost," she said. "Hopefully, once I'm inside, I can find a way to sneak the tiara off his head and get it back to you."

Eva looked uncertain. "I like the party-planner idea," she said, "but it might be dangerous to try to get my tiara. We already know what a horrible mood Jack Frost is in—he could become really nasty."

"Maybe we could fly in as well," Kirsty suggested. "And then, while Rachel is helping Jack Frost, we might be able to grab the tiara without him noticing us."

"Good thinking," Eva said. She waved her wand and announced, "One party planner coming up!"

Rainbow sparkles poured from her wand and swirled around Rachel. When they cleared, Rachel was dressed in bright party clothes and a sparkly wig, carrying bunches of balloons and a bag of party streamers.

Kirsty grinned. "Good luck," she said.
"You, too," Rachel said. "Let's do it!"

Kirsty and Eva fluttered through an open window while Rachel knocked on the door of the castle. When Jack Frost opened it with a suspicious glare, she smiled politely and said, "Hello, I'm from Perfect Party Services. I get the feeling your ball isn't going as planned. Could I offer you some help?"

The frown vanished from Jack Frost's face, and a look of relief appeared in its place. "Yes, please," he said, pushing the door wide open so Rachel could step in. "You're just who I need. Come in, come in."

Kirsty and Eva fluttered to a dark corner of the room and hovered in the shadows. They watched as Rachel showed Jack Frost how to blow up balloons. "Perfect," she said cheerfully, tying neat knots to close the balloons. "And now for the streamers—I have some sparkly ones here," she said, pulling them out of her bag. "These will make the room look fantastic."

While Jack Frost was admiring the streamers and draping them over the gray candleholders on

the walls, Kirsty and Eva jumped at
the chance to fly closer to him. They
swooped down to the table with the
melting ice cream and hid behind it,
waiting for the right moment to grab the
tiara.

The goblins, meanwhile, were getting
bored. One of them threw a scoop of
ice cream at another, giggling as it
splattered on the second goblin's head.

"Hey!" the second goblin grumbled. "Two can play at that game!" And he hurled a lump of ice cream back. It wasn't long before all the goblins were throwing ice cream around the room, making a terrible mess.

Jack Frost was busy arranging his new streamers and ignored them. Then, as he walked closer to the food table to pin up some of the balloons, Kirsty and Rachel exchanged meaningful glances.

"Now!" Eva whispered, and she and

Kirsty both zoomed out of their hiding
place and up toward the tiara
on Jack Frost's head.
Unfortunately
for the fairies,
Kirsty was hit
by the flying ice
cream as they
were fluttering
through the air.
She let out a
squeak of
shock.

"Hey," called
a goblin. "I just saw a fairy. Two
fairies!"

Kirsty and Eva swerved away in fright
as the goblins began chasing them

around the room. One goblin, who
wasn't looking where he
was going, crashed
into Jack Frost
and sent him
skidding
through an
ice-cream
puddle on
the floor.

"Behave yourselves!"
Jack Frost roared
at the goblins.
"You're ruining
this ball!"

Rachel's eyes widened as she
caught sight of Kirsty and Eva being
chased.

She lifted a corner of the tablecloth, and motioned to the panicky fairies to hide under there. "But we saw some fairies," one of the goblins declared to Jack Frost. "We're trying to get rid of them for you."

"Fairies?" thundered Jack Frost, and Rachel trembled at the anger in his voice.

"I . . . I think they went that way," Rachel said quickly, pointing out the window. She desperately hoped that he would believe her.

Immediately, Jack Frost ran outside

in search of the fairies, with the goblins following. Eva and Kirsty flew out from their hiding place, their hearts pounding. "That didn't work very well," Rachel said.

Eva waved her wand at Rachel, turning her back into a fairy. "We need to think of a new plan," she said, but quickly stopped as she heard the sound of footsteps returning.

"Jack Frost's coming back," she hissed. "Quick—hide!"

Trapped in Chains

The fairies dove behind the ice-cream
bowls again as the door swung open
with a crash. Jack Frost stomped back
inside. He looked around and gave an
enormous sigh. "Even the party planner
has had enough of my ball," he said
sadly. He sat on his throne looking
thoroughly fed up as he stared at the
mess the goblins had made.

Kirsty and Rachel were surprised that they actually felt sorry for Jack Frost. They'd been looking forward to the ball at the Golden Palace, so they could imagine how disappointed he must feel, now that his own ball had gone wrong. Even his stylish dress coat was covered in ice cream from when he'd fallen over.

"I wonder if . . ." Kirsty began in a low voice, then shook her head. "No," she said in the next breath, "I don't think it would work."

"What?" Eva whispered.

"Well, I was just wondering if there was any chance we could hold another Fairyland Ball and invite Jack Frost to come this time," Kirsty said. "But I know he doesn't deserve to go, after everything he's done."

Eva gazed at Jack Frost, her head tilted thoughtfully. "I don't know if we can trust him to behave," she said doubtfully. "He might just try to ruin everything again."

"Maybe the thought of dancing, delicious food, and lots of fun will persuade him to be nice," Rachel suggested. "He'd have to give up the tiara first, of course."

"Absolutely," Eva agreed. "And apologize, too. Let's see what he thinks."

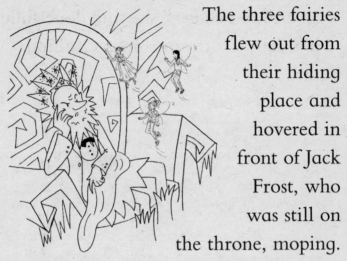

The three fairies flew out from their hiding place and hovered in front of Jack Frost, who was still on the throne, moping.

"Hi, there," Kirsty began timidly. "We were just wondering if you might . . ."

But before she could get any further, Jack Frost clutched the tiara to his head with a look of panic. "You're not getting *this* back," he hissed. Then he fired three bursts of icy magic at the fairies. *Zap! Zap! Zap!*

One of the ice bolts hit a chain of
streamers that then fell down from
the ceiling, landing on the fairies and
forcing them to the ground. The fairies
lay on the cold stone floor and struggled
to get out of the paper chains as Jack
Frost approached. Icy magic crackled
from his fingertips.

Eva wrestled her wand free and
quickly pointed it at Jack Frost,
muttering a magic spell. Glittery sparkles
began to whirl
around his head
so fast that
Jack Frost
couldn't see
the fairies.
"What I
was trying
to tell you,"
Kirsty called
up while he was busy zapping the
sparkles away with ice bolts, "was that
we want to invite you to a Fairyland
Ball."

"I'll clean up your new outfit so you
can show it off," Eva went on, "and

there will be dancing, and the Fairyland Orchestra will play beautiful music. . . ."

"There will be fabulous food, too," Rachel said, as melted ice cream dripped loudly off the tables onto the floor.

Jack Frost looked excited for a moment, but then his expression became suspicious. "That sounds too good to be true," he muttered darkly. "What's the catch?"

"All you have to do," Kirsty told him, "is apologize to Eva and hand back her tiara. What do you think?"

An Extra Guest

There were a tense few moments while the fairy friends waited for Jack Frost's response. Kirsty and Rachel were expecting him to sneer at their offer. They braced themselves for more bolts of icy magic to come their way. But to their surprise, he just nodded eagerly.

"Sorry," he muttered through gritted teeth. He scooped the paper chains off the fairies, then held the tiara out to Eva. "All right, you can have it back, I guess," he grumbled.

Eva beamed as she shook out her wings and fluttered into the air. Kirsty and Rachel flew up, too, glad to be free once more. Eva gave her wand an expert whirl and the tiara shrank down to fairy-size, zipped through the air, and then landed neatly on Eva's head. She put a hand up to touch it and looked happier than Kirsty and Rachel had ever seen her. "Thank you,"

she said, bending into a polite curtsy to
Jack Frost. "That was the right thing
to do. Now I have my magic back, and
I can use it to make a night we'll all
remember! Let me see . . . I'll do outfits
first."

She waved her wand in Jack Frost's direction and the ice-cream stains vanished from his coat, much to his delight. Then she waved her wand at Kirsty and Rachel, and their clothes transformed into the most beautiful ball gowns they'd ever seen. Rachel was now wearing a lilac gown with gathered folds of silk, and Kirsty wore a pink gown with layers of yellow tulle. Both girls had matching tiaras woven with rosebuds and sparkling silver jewels.

"You look just like a princess," Kirsty marveled, gazing at Rachel.

"So do you!" Rachel replied happily.
Eva smiled proudly at their words.
"Now to make our way to the Fairyland
Palace," she said. "Let's go outside
and I'll rustle up the perfect form of
transportation to take us there."

Outside, the goblins had given up

hunting for fairies and were throwing snowballs at one another. With another wave of her wand, Eva conjured up a glass horse-drawn carriage. It looked just like the one the Princess Fairies had taken to the palace for the ball at the start of the girls' adventure. The four white horses wore purple and gold harnesses with matching feathery plumes on their heads.

"Cool!" marveled one of the goblins. "Is that for us?"

"There's not enough room for you, I'm afraid," Eva replied, "but you can follow behind us on these." She waved her wand again, and some magnificent golden sleds appeared on the snow. The goblins whooped with excitement and ran over to them. One goblin even managed to remember to say "Thank you!"

Kirsty, Rachel, Eva, and Jack Frost climbed into the glass carriage, and the four horses began trotting carefully through the snow.

"You're like a fairy godmother, Eva," Rachel said, unable to stop smiling. "This is all so wonderful."

"I guess it might be all right," Jack Frost agreed, fingering his bow tie. "With someone as handsome as me there!"

It didn't take the horses long to arrive at the palace, and as the carriage came to a stop, the palace doors burst open. Down the marble steps hurried King

Oberon, Queen
Titania, and
the six other
Princess Fairies.
They were all
overjoyed to
see the safe
return of
Kirsty,
Rachel,
and Eva.

The three friends
climbed out and said
hello, but Jack Frost stayed in the
carriage, looking awkward. He wasn't
sure that the other fairies would
welcome him.

"I have my tiara back, and I'd like to
throw a ball for everyone to celebrate,"

Eva declared. "And the guests of honor will be Kirsty and Rachel, who have helped us so bravely and kindly."

"Hooray!" the other fairies cheered.

Kirsty felt her cheeks turn red. "It was fun," she said. "Thanks for asking us."

"We've invited an extra guest to the ball," Rachel said. "Someone who's had a change of heart recently. Jack Frost!"

A chorus of gasps and whispers came from the fairies as Jack Frost clambered out of the carriage and stood before them. The smiles had vanished from everyone's faces.

"Are you sure he can be trusted?" King Oberon asked suspiciously. Kirsty and Rachel held their breath. Was their plan of inviting Jack Frost about to go horribly wrong?

Having a Ball

Jack Frost glared at the king and queen. Then he swallowed hard.

"I'm sorry," he muttered. "I promise I will be on my best behavior for the ball. So will the goblins."

The king and queen exchanged a glance, and Queen Titania gave a little nod. "In that case, you're welcome here," she said.

Princess Eva raised her wand once more. "Let the ball begin!" she declared.

It wasn't long before the ball was in full swing. The Fairyland Orchestra played wonderful music, and everyone wore their best clothes and danced all evening. Some of the Dance Fairies helped Kirsty and Rachel practice their ballroom dance steps until they both felt confident about their footwork.

True to their promise, Jack Frost and the goblins behaved themselves. They even showed fairly good table manners when the feast was served, with only a small food fight while the plates were being cleared away. And Princess Eva was the perfect hostess, using her magic to make sure that everyone had a fantastic time.

Then, as the clock struck midnight, the music stopped, and the king, the queen, and the Princess Fairies all approached Kirsty and Rachel.

"It's time for you to return to your own world," Queen Titania said, taking Kirsty and Rachel by their hands. "Thank you again—and we hope to see you soon."

"And enjoy the ball at the Golden Palace," Eva added with a smile. "I have a feeling it's going to be every bit as enchanting as this one."

Rachel and Kirsty were barely able to

say good-bye to all
their fairy friends
before they were
lifted into a magical,
sparkly whirlwind
that took them back
to the Golden
Palace. They
found
themselves
in their
bedroom
again, still
wearing the
beautiful ball
gowns and tiaras Eva had given them.

"Look at our party dresses—they're
perfect now," Rachel said, pulling hers
out of the wardrobe. "Eva must have

used her magic to make them as good as
new again."

"I'm still going to keep my ball gown on, aren't you?" Kirsty said, twirling happily in front of the mirror.

"Definitely," Rachel replied. "Come on, let's go downstairs. The grand ball should be starting any minute." She giggled. "I feel every bit as princessy as the Princess Fairies themselves, going to our second ball of the night," she said. "Especially dressed like this!"

Kirsty and Rachel made their way down to the ballroom where lots of people were already dancing. Kirsty was sure she spotted some extra sparkly lights around the room that hadn't been there before—and the ceiling seemed to be decorated with tiny twinkling stars, too! She wondered with a smile if they were thanks to Eva's magic.

The music sounded great and everyone was enjoying themselves as they danced. Nobody was stepping on anyone's toes, and no one was tripping over anything. The girls knew it was because Princess Eva had her magic tiara back. Hooray for fairy magic!

"We've had so much fun here," Kirsty said, waving to some of the other kids who were wearing dresses almost as pretty as hers. "I'm going to be sad to leave the Golden Palace tomorrow."

"Me too," Rachel said, gazing around at Caroline and Louis; Mrs. King, the palace cook; and Jean, the animal keeper. They were all dressed in their finest and dancing happily. "But I'm sure this won't be the last of our fairy adventures, Kirsty." She grinned.

"Now . . . may I have this dance?"

Laughing, Kirsty took Rachel's hand.
"You may," she replied in her best
princess voice. And the two girls spun
onto the dance floor together.

Rachel and Kirsty have helped all seven
of the Princess Fairies find their tiaras.
Now it's time for them to help

Florence
the Friendship Fairy!

Join their next adventure
in this special sneak peek. . . .

Magic Memories

Rachel Walker pulled a large scrapbook from underneath Kirsty Tate's bed, and the two best friends opened it between them. It was their memory book, full of souvenirs from all the exciting times they'd shared together.

"That vacation on Rainspell Island

was really special," Rachel said, pointing at the ferry tickets and map that had been stuck inside.

"I know," Kirsty replied, smiling. "It was the first time we met each other—and the first time we met the fairies, too!" She lowered her voice. "I wonder if we'll have a fairy adventure this week."

"I hope so," Rachel said, feeling her heart thump excitedly at the thought. She was spending her school vacation with Kirsty's family, and had been wondering the same thing herself. Somehow, extra-special things always seemed to happen when she and Kirsty got together!

The girls kept looking through their book. There was the museum pamphlet from the day they'd met Storm the Lightning Fairy; tickets to Strawberry Farms, where they'd helped Georgia the Guinea Pig Fairy; plus all sorts of photos, postcards, maps, petals, and leaves. . . .

Kirsty frowned as she spotted an empty space on one page. "Did a picture fall out?" she wondered.

"It must have," Rachel said. "You can see that something was stuck there before. I think it was a picture of the fairy models we painted the day we met Willow the Wednesday Fairy. I wonder where it went."

As the girls turned more pages, they realized that photo wasn't the only thing missing. A map of the constellations that Kirsty's gran had given them the night they'd helped Stephanie the Starfish

Fairy had vanished, and so had the all-access pass they'd had for the Fairyland Olympics. Each time they turned a page, they discovered something even worse.

"Oh, no! This photo of us at Camp Stargaze is torn," Rachel said in dismay.

"This page has scribbles all over it," Kirsty cried. "How did that happen?"

"And where did *this* picture come from?" Rachel asked, pointing at a colorful image of a pretty little fairy. She had shoulder-length blonde hair that was pinned back with a pink, star-shaped clip. She wore a sparkly lilac top and a ruffled blue skirt with a colorful belt, and pink sparkly ankle boots. "I've never even seen her before!" She bit her lip. "Something weird is going on, Kirsty. You don't think—"

Before Rachel could finish her sentence, the picture of the fairy began to sparkle and glitter with all the colors of the rainbow. The girls watched, wide-eyed, as the fairy fluttered her wings, stretched, and then flew right off the page in a whirl of twinkling dust!

RAINBOW magic™

There's Magic in Every Series!

The Rainbow Fairies
The Weather Fairies
The Jewel Fairies
The Pet Fairies
The Fun Day Fairies
The Petal Fairies
The Dance Fairies
The Music Fairies
The Sports Fairies
The Party Fairies
The Ocean Fairies
The Night Fairies
The Magical Animal Fairies
The Princess Fairies

Read them all!

SCHOLASTIC

www.scholastic.com
www.rainbowmagiconline.com

HIT entertainment

RMFAIRY